This book belongs to

_____

PEOPLE AT WORK

WALT DISNEY FUN-TO-LEARN LIBRARY

A BANTAM BOOK
NEW YORK · TORONTO · LONDON · SYDNEY · AUCKLAND

ISBN 0-553-05520-8

Published simultaneously in the United States and Canada. Bantam Books are published by Bantam Books, Inc. Its trademark, consisting of the words "Bantam Books" and the portrayal of a rooster, is Registered in U.S. Patent and Trademark Office and in other countries. Marca Registrada. Bantam Books, Inc., 666 Fifth Avenue, New York, New York 10103. Printed in the United States of America. 19 18 17 16 15 14 13 12 11 10

Classic® binding, R. R. Donnelley & Sons Company. U.S. Patent No. 4,408,780; Patented in Canada 1984; Patents in other countries issued or pending.

It's morning, and everyone is getting up. Everywhere, people are getting ready to do their jobs. All the different jobs people do are important, because almost everything we eat, wear, use, live in, or enjoy, is made somewhere by someone.

Some people have jobs in factories or stores or office buildings. Some people work at home. Some people have jobs helping other people.

Maybe it's snowing.

Maybe it's raining.

But most people get to their jobs no matter what.

Let's see what some of those jobs are.

There's a fire on Tenth Street!
The fire fighters slide down the pole
and jump onto the fire trucks.

Ding! Ding! Out of the way!
Here's the fire. Get out the hoses!

It was just a pot roast burning. Nothing serious.

Back to the fire station to get the trucks ready for the next alarm.

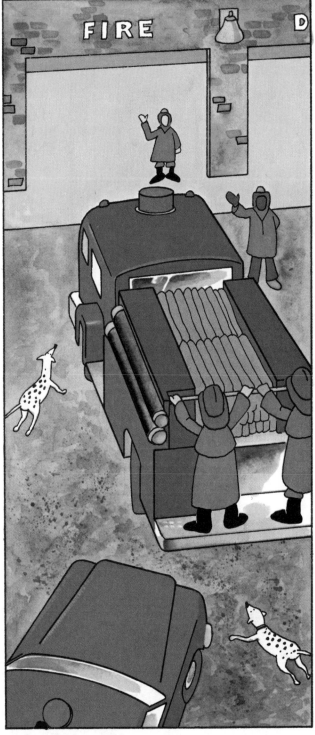

Doctors and nurses take care of people when they are sick. They also help people take care of themselves when they are healthy.

Huey, Dewey, and Louie are getting their checkups. The doctor looks down Dewey's throat. He weighs and measures Huey, and he gives Louie a shot to help him stay healthy.

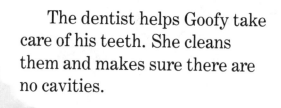

The dentist helps Goofy take care of his teeth. She cleans them and makes sure there are no cavities.

Sometimes, people get sick and have to go to the hospital. All kinds of people work in a hospital. There are doctors, and nurses, and X-ray technicians, and nurse's aides, and ambulance drivers. These people all help make sure that the patients get well.

Police officers help people in many different ways.
Chief O'Hara patrols the streets to keep them safe.

He directs traffic and makes sure that everyone crosses
the street safely.

Morty and Ferdie are going to
the library because they want to
borrow some books. The librarian
helps Morty find a book about
animals. Ferdie wants
a book of riddles.

Houses and apartments are built by people called builders. These builders are building a new house for Minnie. First the workers dig a big hole and then they pour in the concrete to make the foundation. Trucks take away all the dirt and bring back the wood the builders will need to make the walls.

WELCOME

BLUE PRINT

Then a bricklayer builds the chimney, the roofer puts the shingles on the roof, the carpenters put up the walls and put in the windows and doors, the plumber puts in all the pipes, and the electrician puts in all the wires. The paperhanger and the painter come to put up the wallpaper and paint the rooms. Minnie chooses the colors she wants in her living room.

All the things we use are made somewhere by someone. People who work in factories make the clothes we buy in the store.

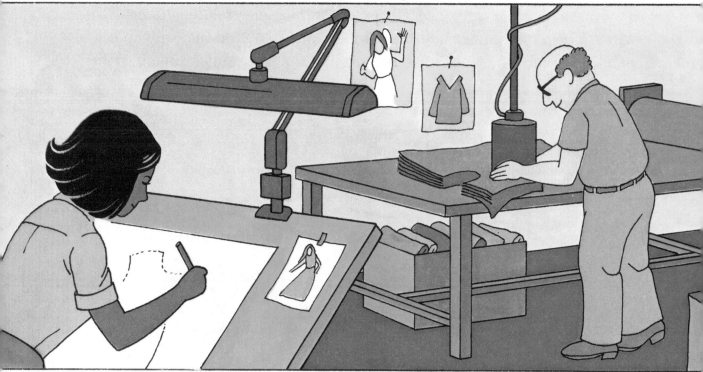

A designer makes the pattern, a cutter cuts out the material, and a sewer sews all the pieces together.

In a car factory, the workers put together the cars on a long, moving assembly line.

They put the body of the car together. Then they put in the motor and put on the wheels. The finished car is driven off the assembly line. Donald can hardly wait to buy one!

People who work in the department store sell all kinds of things that are made in factories.

Mickey and his friends are out shopping today. Minnie tries on some new clothes. Daisy buys some makeup.

Morty and Ferdie and Donald's nephews look at the toys. And Goofy wants a fine new pair of shoes.

When something you buy breaks, someone has to fix it. The worker who works in the repair shop can fix that toaster for Donald.

The washing machine repairman comes and fixes the washing machine right in Donald's house.

When the pipes in Goofy's house leak,
the plumber stops the water from spilling all
over Goofy's kitchen.

The gas station is a kind of repair shop, too. The garage
mechanics fix your car, change the oil or the tires, or "fill 'er up"
with gasoline. A truck driver delivers the gasoline that you buy
at the gas station.

GAS

Some people drive cars when they want to go somewhere. But sometimes, it's easier to take a bus, a taxicab, a train, or a plane.

Goofy is going to take the bus. He pays his fare to the bus driver. Donald is late. He is going to take a taxi.

Mickey is going on a train trip. He buys his ticket from the ticket clerk and gets on the train. The engineer drives the engine that pulls the train cars into the station.

When Mickey finds a seat, the conductor comes and punches his ticket. The conductor calls out the names of the different stations so that people will know when to get off.

Donald is taking Huey on an airplane trip to visit Uncle Scrooge. Many different people work at the airport. They help the passengers get safely and comfortably to the right places — with all their luggage.

Donald buys the tickets from the ticket clerk and gets the luggage weighed.

Then the baggage clerk puts the suitcases on a truck.

The baggage handler loads the baggage on the plane.

Food is loaded onto the plane, too. The flight attendant welcomes everyone on bo:

The pilot prepares to take off. "Fasten your seat belts, please."
The flight attendant serves Donald and Huey their lunch.

The farmer grows vegetables in the fields. You can see
lettuce and string beans and tomatoes and corn.

The farmer harvests wheat for bread.

Apples and pears have to be picked.

The milk we drink comes from cows.

Chickens lay the eggs we eat for breakfast.

And all this food is driven to the market, and to
places where some foods are put in special packages.

In a frozen-food factory, the fresh meat, fish, and vegetables are put in packages and frozen before they go to the store.

Some foods are cooked and put in cans. This way, they will stay fresh for a long time.

Some foods, like breakfast cereals, are mixed in the factory. On their class trip, Morty and Ferdie see the cereal go into boxes.

Truck drivers deliver the packages, cans, and boxes to stores in every neighborhood.

Daisy goes shopping in a supermarket that sells all kinds of
food. Truck drivers deliver food from the farms and the food factories.
People who work in the store unload it and put it on the shelves.
Daisy picks out the foods she wants. Then she will pay the cashier
who works in the front of the store.

Some stores sell special things, or things that were made right in the store.

The baker makes cakes and breads and cookies at the bakery.

The toy store owner sells toys, and sometimes makes them, too.

The pharmacist in the drug store mixes the medicines so they are ready to sell.

Mail is very important. Many people work together to make sure that all the letters and packages get to the right places.

Huey, Dewey, and Louie are writing a letter to Grandma Duck.

The mail carrier picks up the letter from the mailbox and takes it to the post office.

The mail sorters sort the letters. They make sure that Grandma's letter is sent to the right town.

A truck driver drives the mailbags to the post office in Grandma's town.

There, Grandma Duck's mail carrier delivers the letter right to her mailbox.

"What a nice letter!"

Books tell us all kinds of important things. They show us how the world works, and they help us enjoy our quiet times.

Writers write the books.

The people who work at the printers use big presses on which the pages of the book are printed.

The binders put the pages together to make up the book you buy in the store.

Everyone loves to read good books.

At school, the teacher is teaching Huey, Dewey, and Louie how to read books. Dewey likes storybooks. Louie likes books about animals. They have fun learning how to count and how to write letters on the blackboard.

Aa Bb Cc
Dd Ee

Huey, Dewey, and Louie enjoy going to school because their teacher tells them so many exciting things. Today, Louie is finding out all about lions.

Some people entertain us. Actors and dancers and musicians and clowns and singers make us laugh and feel good.

The stage crew in the theater helps with the lights, the costumes, and the makeup. Stagehands move the scenery and pull the curtains up and down.

And the people in the audience clap their hands and have fun.

Actors and dancers also make television shows. And so do newspeople. All kinds of people work at the television studio. There, the person with the camera takes a moving picture of the people in the television show.

Then the show is broadcast from the television station. If you turn on your television set, you can watch the show at home.

Some people make beautiful things for us to look at. They are called artists.

Painters paint pictures.

Sculptors make statues.

People like to go to museums and look at all the beautiful things artists have been busy making.

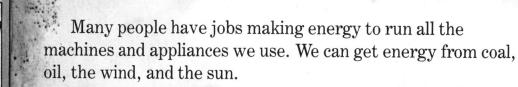

Many people have jobs making energy to run all the machines and appliances we use. We can get energy from coal, oil, the wind, and the sun.

Coal miners are the people who dig coal. Truck drivers take the coal to the generating plant. There the coal is burned to make steam. The big generators turn this steam into electricity.

In our homes, we need electricity to light the lights and run the refrigerator, the toaster, the record player—and many other things, too. Please turn off the lights and the record player when you leave the room, Huey.

At the end of the day, when all the work is done, it is time to clean up. Every day, people throw out garbage. The sanitation worker will come early the next morning to take it away.

In the house, it's time to clean up, too. Morty and Ferdie
help Mickey after a long day.

Now that you have seen some of the different jobs there are,
can you see how important each one is? Children have jobs that
are important, too. Everybody helps everybody else. That's
what makes life so interesting, and so much fun.